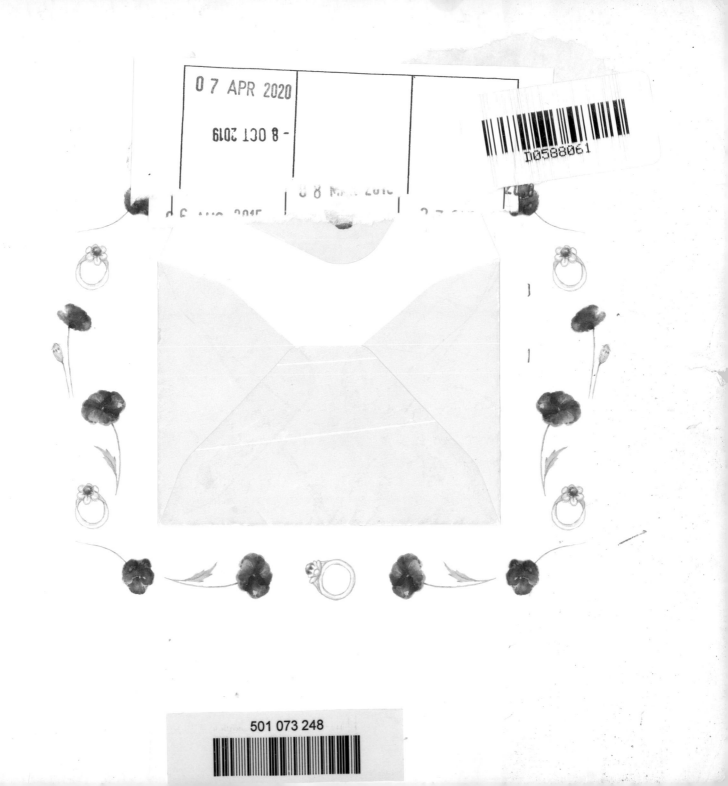

Honeypot Hill

To the City

The Orchards

Saffron Thimble's Sewing Shop

Paddle Steamer Quay

Aunt Marigold' General Store

Lavender Valley Garden Centre

Healing House and Garden

The Worthingtons' House

Lavender Lake

Bumble Bee's Teashop

Lavender Lake School of Dance

Hedgerows Hotel
Where Mimosa lives

SCHOOL

Peppermint Pond

Rosehip School

Summer Meadow

Christmas Corner

Wildspice Woods

Join Princess Poppy on more adventures . . .

★ The Birthday ★

★ Ballet Shoes ★

★ Twinkletoes ★

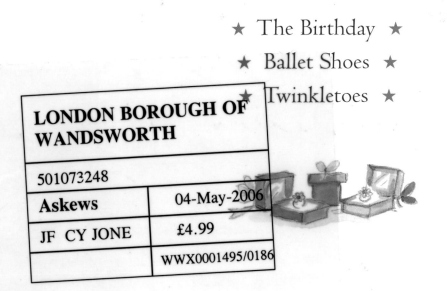

THE FAIR DAY BALL
A PICTURE CORGI BOOK 978 0 552 55338 4 (from January 2007)
0 552 55338 7

First published in Great Britain by Picture Corgi,
an imprint of Random House Children's Books

This edition published 2006

1 3 5 7 9 10 8 6 4 2

Text copyright © Janey Louise Jones, 2006
Illustration copyright © Picture Corgi Books, 2006
Illustrations by Veronica Vasylenko
Design by Tracey Cunnell

Picture Corgi Books are published by Random House Children's Books,
61–63 Uxbridge Road, London W5 5SA, a division of The Random House Group Ltd,
London, Sydney, Auckland, Johannesburg and agencies throughout the world.
THE RANDOM HOUSE GROUP Limited Reg. No. 954009
www.kidsatrandomhouse.co.uk
www.princesspoppy.com

A CIP catalogue record for this book is available from the British Library.

Printed in China

Princess Poppy

The Fair Day Ball

Written by Janey Louise Jones

PICTURE CORGI

For Evie and Faye,
who were the first little princesses
to love Poppy

★

You are cordially invited
to
The Fair Day Ball
at
Cornsilk Castle

Dress code:
princes and princesses

The Fair Day Ball

featuring

Dad

★

Princess Poppy

Honey

★

Saffron

★

David Sage

★

Mum

★

Granny Bumble

★

Holly Mallow

★

"Today, you *shall* go to the Fair, and you *shall* go to the Fair Day Ball at Cornsilk Castle," Poppy said to herself in her best Fairy Godmother voice as she twirled in front of her mirror and tapped her reflection with her love-heart wand.

"Time to leave for the Fair!" called her dad.

Soon they could see the pink and white striped stalls and the fairground.

"There's Honey," said Poppy, as she spotted her best friend running towards them.

"Oh Poppy, look at the ponies on the carousel – shall we have a go?" said Honey, pointing in the direction of the ride.

"Dad, please can we ride on the carousel? Pleeeeease?" asked Poppy.

"Of course you can, it is Fair Day after all."

"And then can we have some ice cream?" said Poppy.

"We'll see," smiled Poppy's dad.

BUMBLE'S CAKES

FORTUNE TELLING

Poppy and Honey climbed onto the beautiful silver ponies, giggling with delight. They had one ride. Then another. And another!

"Again, Dad! Again!" begged Poppy.

"That's enough now, girls," Granny Bumble called over from the Blossom Bakehouse stall. "Don't forget, you've got all day . . ."

"I think she's right," said Poppy's dad, handing them both fresh cream strawberry ices drizzled with chocolate and honey.

"Mmmmm, deeeelicious! Thank you!" chorused Poppy and Honey.

"Dad, can we go round the Fair now?" asked Poppy.

"Off you go then," said Dad.

Everyone was at the Fair.
Mum waved from her hat stall . . .

Cousin Saffron waved too – not
from her sewing stall, but from their
teacher Holly Mallow's jewellery stall.

They also saw Saffron's boyfriend,
the vet, David Sage, at his pet stall.

Then Poppy spotted the most gorgeous dress on Saffron's stall.
It was made from layers of white tulle, with poppies stitched all
over the skirt. It was quite simply PERFECT! She had to have it!

"Saffron, I'd like to buy that dress," said Poppy, as she reached
into her purse. But she only had a few pennies.

"I'd love you to have it, Poppy, but it took ages to make.
I'm afraid that's not enough money," said Saffron softly.

"Dad, please can I have it? Pleeeease?" begged Poppy.

"You've already had lots of special treats today . . ." said Dad.

Saffron's Sewing Stall

"If you don't have the money, you can't have the dress," explained Mum.

"That's *not fair!*" grumped Poppy, stamping her foot. "I *need* the dress for the ball tonight." Honey nodded in sympathy, because *she* wanted the golden honey-coloured dress.

"Why don't you earn the princess dresses by helping out on some stalls?" suggested Mum.

"Aw, I'm too tired . . ." said Poppy, "and I won't know what to do."

But Mum was not going to change her mind.

First they helped out at Saffron's stall.

"You can help me fold these chiffons and muslins," she suggested, "and when you've finished you can go and help Miss Mallow."

"This is so unfair – I hate working!" Poppy grumbled.

"Me too," said Honey, "but I do so want that amazing dress."

They didn't want to admit it, but it was actually quite fun.

"Let's go and help Miss Mallow now," suggested Poppy.

"Hello, princess helpers!" cried Holly. "Can you tie bows on these little ring boxes for me, please?"

"OK then," Poppy said. "Come on, Honey."

At the end of the day, Poppy and Honey were still hard at work.

"You must be exhausted, girls! I thought you might need some of Aunt Marigold's cloudy lemonade," said Mum. "You have both worked really hard. I am very proud of you. So now, I promise, you *shall* go to the ball and maybe you'll even get to wear princess dresses."

As night fell, Poppy's mum and dad took Poppy and Honey
to the courtyard gates in front of Cornsilk Castle. Dad held
a candle near the big sycamore tree and called the girls over.
Poppy and Honey peered into the candle-lit branches.
"Princess baskets!" cried Poppy.

Inside the satin-lined baskets there were necklaces, floral tiaras, perfume, lip cream and . . . best of all, the princess dresses. The girls could hardly believe their eyes.

"Oh, thank you!" said Poppy. "Let's go to the castle and get changed."

"We are DEFINITELY princesses now," Poppy told her best friend, as they twirled around together.

They walked into the Great Hall of the castle, which was decorated with flickering candles and petals scattered all over the dance floor.

But Poppy and Honey only had eyes for Saffron, as she floated around the dance floor with David, looking like a fairy princess in a soft, white chiffon dress. She wore satin sandals tied with ribbons at her ankles, and a circle of moonstones at her neck.

"Doesn't she look just like Cinderella?" Poppy whispered to Honey.

"And he is Prince Charming!" giggled Honey.

Just then, the music stopped . . .

David knelt down on one knee and took Saffron's hand.

"Saffron, will you marry me?"

"Oh David, I would love to!" blushed Saffron.

David kissed her hand and slipped a sparkly flower-shaped diamond ring onto her finger.

Poppy and Honey held hands and danced round in a circle. "Hurrah!" they cried. "A wedding in Honeypot Hill! It's a dream come true!"

"Poppy! Honey! Come over!" called
Saffron. The two little friends stopped
spinning and walked shyly towards her,
holding hands.

"Girls, you are such beautiful,
hardworking and helpful princesses —
will you be flower girls at my wedding?"
said Saffron.

"We would love to!" Poppy breathed.

"Thank you!" whispered Honey.

When it was time to go home, Poppy said, "Dad, I will *never* be greedy again. But I just can't help wondering if I *might* get a new dress for Saffron's wedding?"

Mum and Dad laughed and hugged their special little princess.